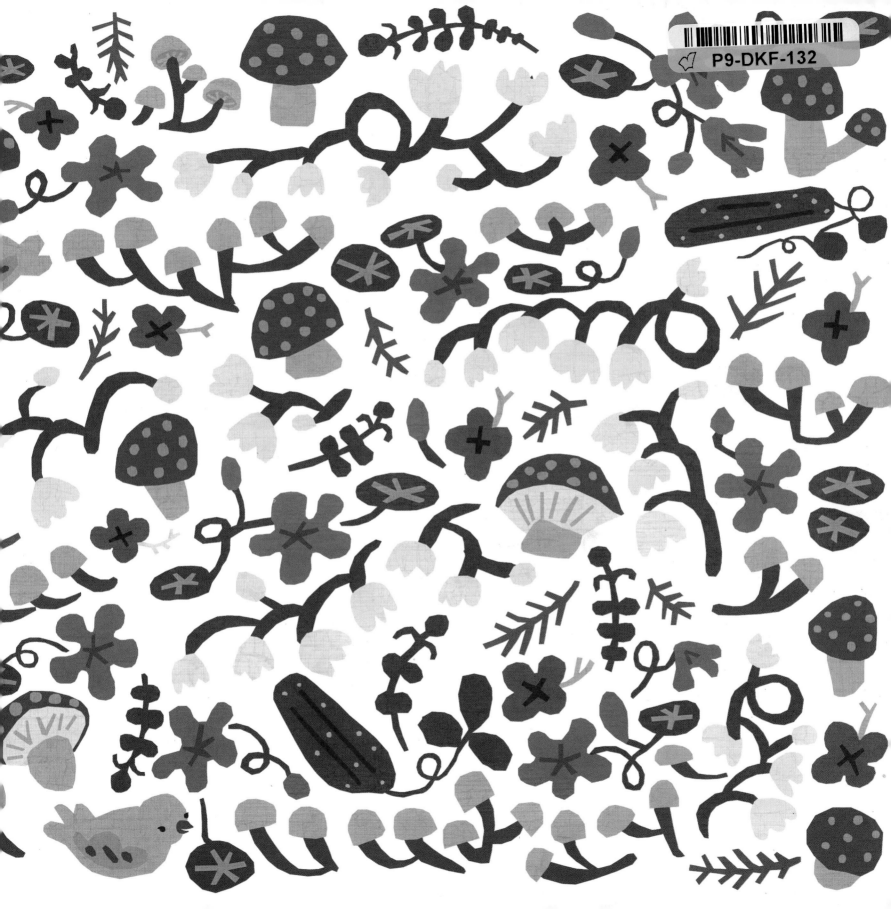

For the dreamers—K.B.

Published in 2021 by Cameron + Company, a division of ABRAMS.

Library of Congress Cataloging-in-Publication Data available.
ISBN: 978-1-951836-27-6

Printed in China

10 9 8 7 6 5 4 3 2 1

Cameron Kids is an imprint of Cameron + Company

Cameron + Company
Petaluma, California
www.cameronbooks.com

IF YOU
ARE THE
DREAMER

KRISTEN BALOUCH

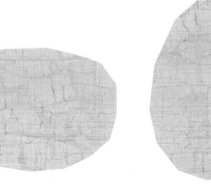

cameron kids

If you are the egg,
I am the hen.

If you are the bear,
I am the den.

If you are the pilot,
I am the plane.

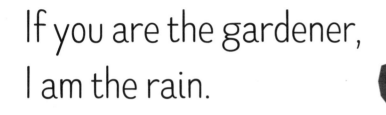

If you are the gardener,
I am the rain.

If you are the surfer,
I am the swell.

If you are the snail,
I am the shell.

If you are the squirrel,
I am the tree.

If you are the traveler,
I am the sea.

If you are the writer,
I am the nook.

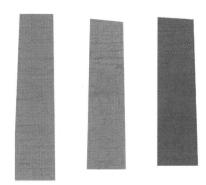

If you are the reader,
I am the book.

And, if you are the dreamer . . . .

I am the stars
holding your dreams,
whatever they are.